"But if I'm all this," said the Leopard, "why didn't you go spotty too?"

"Oh, plain black's best for a man," said the Ethiopian. "Now come along and we'll see if we can get even with Mr. One-Two-Three-Where's-your-Breakfast!"

So they went away and lived happily ever afterwards, Best Beloved. That is all.

Oh, now and then you will hear grown-ups say, "Can the Ethiopian change his skin or the Leopard his spots?" I don't think even grown-ups would keep on saying such a silly thing if the Leopard and the Ethiopian hadn't done it once—do you? But they will never do it again, Best Beloved. They are quite contented as they are.

"I 'll make them with the tips of my fingers," said the Ethiopian. "There's plenty of black left on my skin still. Stand over!"

Then the Ethiopian put his five fingers close together (there was plenty of black left on his new skin still) and pressed them all over the Leopard, and wherever the five fingers touched they left five little black marks, all close together. You can see them on any Leopard's skin you like. Sometimes the fingers slipped and the marks got a little blurred; but if you look closely at any Leopard you will see that there are always five spots—off five black finger-tips.

"Now you **are** a beauty!" said the Ethiopian. "You can lie out on the bare ground and look like a heap of pebbles. You can lie on the naked rocks and look like a piece of pudding-stone. You can lie out on a leafy branch and look like sunshine sifting through the leaves; and you can lie right across the centre path and look like nothing in particular. Think of that and purr!"

"Think of Giraffe," said the Ethiopian. "Or if you prefer stripes, think of Zebra. They find their spots and stripes give them perfect satisfaction."

"Umm," said the Leopard. "I wouldn't look like Zebra—not for ever so."

"Well, make up your mind," said the Ethiopian, "because I'd hate to go hunting without you, but I must if you insist on looking like a sun-flower against a tarred fence."

"I'll take spots, then," said the Leopard; "but don't make them too vulgar-big. I wouldn't look like Giraffe—not for ever so."

So he changed his skin then and there, and the Leopard was more excited than ever; he had never seen a man change his skin before.

"What about me?" he said, when the Ethiopian had worked his last little finger into his fine new black skin.

"You take Baviaan's advice too. He told you to go into spots."

"So I did," said the Leopard. "I went into other spots as fast as I could. I went into this spot with you, and a lot of good it has done me."

"Oh," said the Ethiopian, "Baviaan didn't mean spots in South Africa. He meant spots on your skin."

"What's the use of that?" said the Leopard.

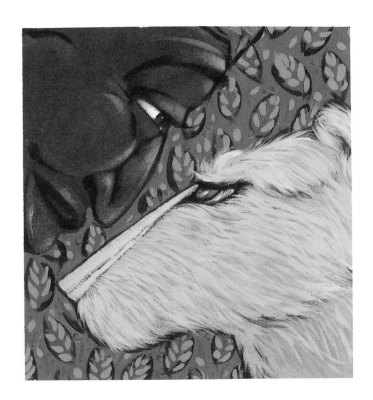

"Well, calling names won't catch dinner," said the Ethiopian. "The long and little of it is that we don't match our backgrounds. I'm going to take Baviaan's advice. He told me I ought to change; and as I've nothing to change except my skin I'm going to change that."

"What to?" said the Leopard, tremendously excited.

"To a nice working blackish-brownish colour, with a little purple in it, and touches of slaty-blue. It will be the very thing for hiding in hollows and behind trees."

They let the Zebra and the Giraffe up; and the Zebra moved away to some little thorn-bushes where the sunlight fell all stripy, and the Giraffe moved off to some tallish trees where the shadows fell all blotchy.

"Now watch," said the Zebra and the Giraffe. "This is the way it's done. One—two—three! And where's your breakfast?"

Leopard stared, and Ethiopian stared, but all they could see were stripy shadows and blotched shadows in the forest, but never a sign of Zebra and Giraffe. They had just walked off and hidden themselves in the shadowy forest.

"Hi! Hi!" said the Ethiopian. "That's a trick worth learning. Take a lesson in it, Leopard. You show up in this dark place like a bar of soap in a coal-scuttle."

"Ho! Ho!" said the Leopard. "Would it surprise you very much to know that you show up in this dark place like a mustard-plaster on a sack of coals?"

The Ethiopian scratched his head and said, "It ought to be 'sclusively a rich fulvous orange-tawny from head to heel, and it ought to be Giraffe; but it is covered all over with chestnut blotches. What have you at **your** end of the table, Brother?"

And the Leopard scratched his head and he said, "It ought to be 'sclusively a delicate greyish-fawn, it ought to be Zebra; but it is covered all over with black and purple stripes. What in the world have you been doing with yourself, Zebra? Don't you know that if you were on the High Veldt I could see you ten miles off? You haven't any form."

"Yes," said the Zebra, "but this isn't the High Veldt. Can't you see?"

"I can now," said the Leopard. "But I couldn't all yesterday. How is it done?"

"Let us up," said the Zebra, "and we will show you."

"For goodness sake," said the Leopard at tea-time, "let us wait till it gets dark. This daylight hunting is a perfect scandal."

So they waited till dark. Then the Leopard heard something breathing sniffily in the starlight that fell all stripy through the branches, and he jumped at the noise. It smelt like Zebra, and it felt like Zebra, and when he knocked it down it kicked like Zebra, but he couldn't see it. So he said, "Be quiet, O you person without a form. I am going to sit on your head until morning, because there is something about you that I don't understand."

Presently he heard a grunt and a crash and a scramble, and the Ethiopian called out, "I've caught a thing that I can't see. It smells like Giraffe, it kicks like Giraffe, but it hasn't any form."

"Don't trust it," said the Leopard. "Sit on its head till morning—same as me. They haven't any form—any of them."

So they sat on them hard till bright morning-time, and then Leopard said, "What have you at your end of the table, Brother?"

"Fiddle!" said the Leopard. "I remember them perfectly on the High Veldt, especially their marrow-bones. Giraffe is about seventeen feet high, golden-yellow from head to heel; Zebra is about four and a half feet high, of a 'sclusively grey-fawn colour."

"Umm," said the Ethiopian, looking into the speckly-spickly shadows of the aboriginal Flora-forest. "Then they ought to show up in dark places like ripe bananas in a smoke-house."

But they didn't. The Leopard and the Ethiopian hunted all day; and though they could smell them and hear them, they never saw one of them.

That puzzled the Leopard and the Ethiopian, but they set off to look for the aboriginal Flora, and presently, after ever so many days, they saw a great, high, tall forest full of tree trunks all 'sclusively speckled and sprottled and spottled, dotted and splashed and slashed and hatched and cross-hatched with shadows. (Say that quickly aloud, and you will see how **very** shadowy the forest must have been.)

"What is this," said the Leopard, "that is so 'sclusively dark, and yet so full of little pieces of light?"

"I don't know," said the Ethiopian, "but it ought to be the aboriginal Flora. I can smell Giraffe, and I can hear Giraffe, but I can't see Giraffe."

"That's curious," said the Leopard. "I suppose it's because we have just come in out of the sunshine. I can smell Zebra, and I can hear Zebra, but I can't see Zebra."

"Wait a bit," said the Ethiopian. "It's a long time since we've hunted them. Perhaps we've forgotten what they were like."

Then said Baviaan, "The game has gone into other spots; and my advice to you, Leopard, is to go into other spots as soon as you can."

And the Ethiopian said, "That is all very fine, but I wish to know whither the aboriginal Fauna has migrated."

Then said Baviaan, "The aboriginal Fauna has joined the aboriginal Flora because it is high time for a change; and my advice to you, Ethiopian, is to change as soon as you can."

They had a beautiful time in the 'sclusively speckly and spickly shadows of the forest, while the Leopard and the Ethiopian ran about over the 'sclusively greyish-yellowish-reddish High Veldt outside, wondering where all their breakfasts and their dinners and their teas had gone. At last they were so hungry that they ate rats and beetles and rock-rabbits, and they had a Big Tummy-ache. And then they met Baviaan, who is Quite the Wisest Animal in All South Africa.

Said Leopard to Baviaan (and it was a very hot day), "Where has all the game gone?"

And Baviaan winked. **He** knew.

Said the Ethiopian to Baviaan, "Can you tell me the present habitat of the aboriginal Fauna?" (That meant just the same thing, Best Beloved, but the Ethiopian always used long words. He was a grown-up.)

And Baviaan winked. **He** knew.

They scuttled for days and days and days till they came to a great forest, 'sclusively full of trees and bushes and stripy, speckly, patchy-blatchy shadows, and there they hid: and after another long time, what with standing half in the shade and half out of it, and what with the slippery-slidy shadows of the trees falling on them, the Giraffe grew blotchy, and the Zebra grew stripy, and the Eland and the Koodoo grew darker, with little wavy grey lines on their backs like bark on a tree trunk; and so, though you could hear them and smell them, you could very seldom see them, and then only when you knew precisely where to look.

And, also, there was an Ethiopian with bows and arrows (a 'sclusively greyish-brownish-yellowish man he was then), who lived on the High Veldt with the Leopard; and the two used to hunt together—the Ethiopian with his bows and arrows, and the Leopard 'sclusively with his teeth and claws—till the Giraffe and the Eland and the Koodoo and the Quagga and all the rest of them didn't know which way to jump. They didn't indeed!

After a long time, they learned to avoid anything that looked like a Leopard or an Ethiopian; and bit by bit, they went away from the High Veldt.

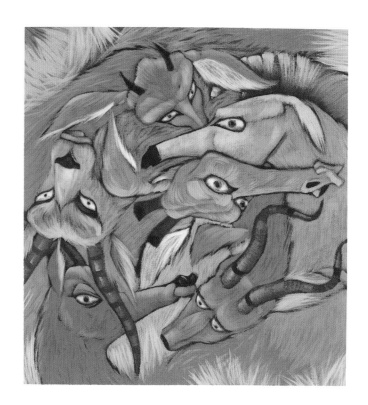

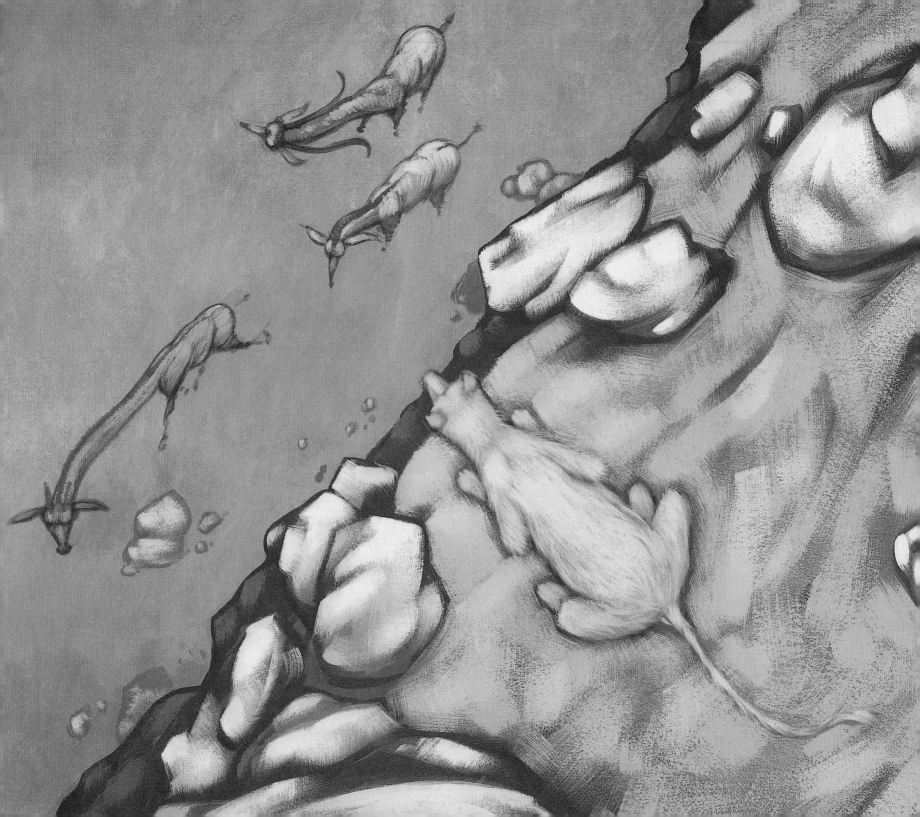

But the Leopard, he was the 'sclusivest sandiest-yellowish-brownest of them all—a greyish-yellowish catty-shaped kind of beast, and he matched the 'sclusively yellowish-greyish-brownish colour of the High Veldt to one hair. This was very bad for the Giraffe and the Zebra and the rest of them; for he would lie down by a 'sclusively yellowish-greyish-brownish stone or clump of grass, and when the Giraffe or the Zebra or the Eland or the Koodoo or the Bush-Buck or the Bonte-Buck came by he would surprise them out of their jumpsome lives. O He would indeed!

In the days when everybody started fair, O Best Beloved, the Leopard lived in a place called the High Veldt. 'Member it wasn't the Low Veldt, or the Bush Veldt, or the Sour Veldt, but the 'sclusively bare, hot, shiny High Veldt, where there was sand and sandy-coloured rock and 'sclusively tufts of sandy-yellowish grass. The Giraffe and the Zebra and the Eland and the Koodoo and the Hartebeest lived there; and they were 'sclusively sandy-yellow-brownish all over;

written by Rudyard Kipling

HOW THE LEOPARD GOT HIS SPOTS

illustrated by Lori Lohstoeter

Rabbit Ears Books

ABDO Publishing Company is the exclusive school and library distributor of Rabbit Ears Books.

Library bound edition 2006.

Copyright © 1995 Rabbit Ears Entertainment, LLC.,
S. Norwalk, Connecticut.

Library of Congress Cataloging-in-Publication Data

Kipling, Rudyard, 1865-1936.
   How the leopard got his spots / written by Rudyard Kipling ; illustrated by Lori Lohstoeter.
      p. cm.
   "Rabbit Ears books."
   Summary: Relates how the leopard got his spotted coat in order to hunt the animals in the dappled shadows of the forest.
   ISBN 1-59679-344-9
   [1. Leopard—Fiction. 2. Animals—Fiction.] I. Lohstoeter, Lori, ill. II. Title.

PZ7.K632Hk 2005
[E]—dc22

                                                            2004066344

All Rabbit Ears books are reinforced library binding
and manufactured in the United States of America.

ABDO
Publishing Company